I0550628

This book belongs to:

_____

First Print. eknlinks.com 2009 © Ken Ninomiya . www.BizEBunch.com . www.rustyslemonadestand.com

Dedication

This book is dedicated to all of the future young business leaders of the world. It is dedicated to the children who have dreams and aspirations of great accomplishment.

Tomorrow's business leaders will face new challenges that may not have yet revealed themselves, but the foundations of a strong business mind supported by unmatched high ethical standards will help future leaders to overcome those challenges.

This book is dedicated to children who overcome any obstacle in life to fulfill their dreams and who will work to change the world.

This book is dedicated to my kids Suki, Rusty, and Chiquita, who are blessed with the promise of a bright future and who are destined to improve our world.

About the Author

Ken Ninomiya was introduced to business at the age of 7 by helping his dad at local flea markets. He opened his first retail store by the age of 18 and since then has helped to develop many business ideas through his strategic management company, ekn links.

Ken holds an MBA and is currently a professor of business and marketing. He created BizEBunch to help explain business concepts to his own children so that they maximize their opportunities for a better life. BizEBunch.com provides a series of books, activities and lessons that help to inspire and educate children about life, family and business.

www.eknlinks.com We can help. If you have an idea or business, let us help to make it shine.

2009 © Ken Ninomiya . www.BizEBunch.com . www.RustysLemonadestand.com

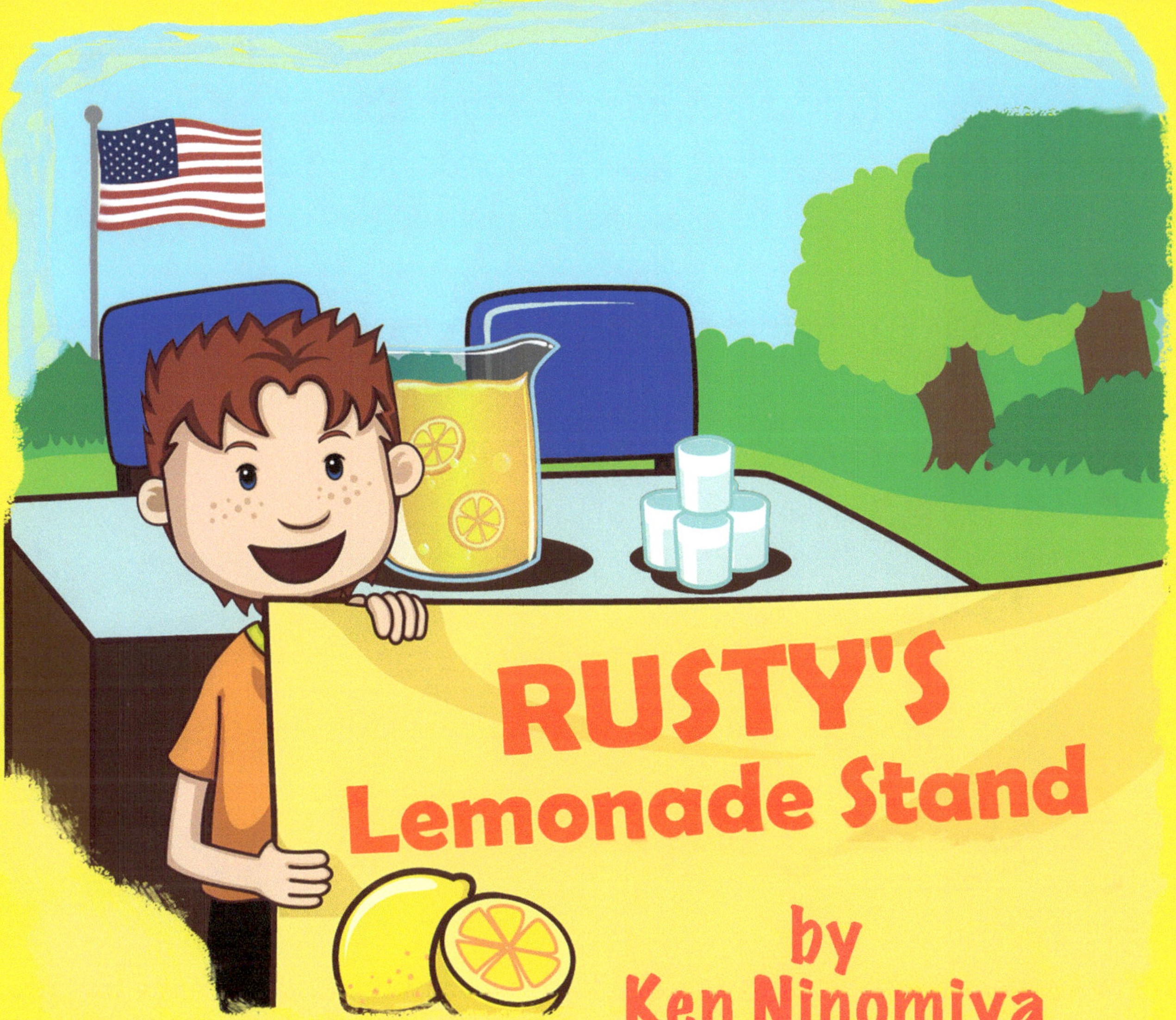

RUSTY'S
Lemonade Stand

by
Ken Ninomiya

2009 © Ken Ninomiya . www.BizEBunch.com . www.rustyslemonadestand.com

Rusty is a smart, ambitious young man. He likes to do many things and stay very active by playing sports. He also loves to play video games.

Rusty wanted to buy the newest video game but did not have enough money. He receives a $5.00 per month allowance for doing all his schoolwork on time and doing some chores around the house.

The new video game that Rusty really, really wanted cost $30.00. Rusty only had $15.00 in his piggy bank. He couldn't wait three more months to buy the game.

How much more money did Rusty need?

2009 © Ken Ninomiya . www.BizEBunch.com . www.rustyslemonadestand.com

Rusty's Thinking Box

The new video game Rusty wants to buy costs $30.00. He only has $15.00. How much more money does Rusty need?

Video Game $ 30.00
Rusty has   – $ 15.00
Rusty needs = $.

Rusty gets $5.00 allowance each month.

How many more months does Rusty have to save his allowance in order to buy the video game?

$5.00 x _____ (more months) = _____

What else can Rusty do to get more money for the video game?

2009 © Ken Ninomiya . www.BizEBunch.com . www.rustyslemonadestand.com

Rusty asked his Dad for the extra money he needed but his Dad said, "No, son. You will have to save up your allowance or earn it another way."

Rusty's Dad suggested that he try to earn the $15.00 he needed to buy the new video game.

Rusty got an allowance for doing his chores around the house. His Dad explained that grown-ups work to earn money to buy things like a house, a car and even video games for their kids. Rusty's Dad explained that to earn enough money to buy the video game he wanted, he could work for him around the house or maybe open up his own business to earn money for himself.

2009 © Ken Ninomiya . www.BizEBunch.com . www.rustyslemonadestand.com

2009 © Ken Ninomiya . www.BizEBunch.com . www.rustyslemonadestand.com

Rusty did not know what a business was. Dad explained that in a business someone does something that they are really good at or sells something they make to earn money.

Rusty remembered that he had been to a business before, like the grocery store and the video game store. These stores were all a business. His Mom and Dad gave them money for something they needed.

Dad also explained that the man who comes to cut the grass on the front lawn has his own business, and even the Doctor's office that Rusty goes to is a business. Rusty thought that everybody had their own business to earn money but him.

A business makes something or sells something to earn money. Consumers give a business money in exchange for something they would like to have.

2009 © Ken Ninomiya . www.BizEBunch.com . www.rustyslemonadestand.com

The next day in school, Rusty's teacher talked about some of the people in history that have made the United States a great place.

Ms. Sam explained that the United States is a great country because anybody can be anything they wanted to be when they grow up, from the President of the United States to an owner of a business.

Rusty asked Ms. Sam why someone would want to be an owner of a business. Ms. Sam explained that the United States has grown into a great country because people just like him wanted to own a business.

Ms. Sam explained that businesses give people things they need like water, food, clothes and homes. Ms. Sam also explained that businesses help others by giving them a place to work to earn money to buy those things they need. She said that businesses help to provide friends and family jobs so people like him can earn money. 5

Rusty's Thinking Box

Can you name a business that you know?

Does anyone in your family work in a business?

Is anyone in your family the boss of a business?

Do you want to work in a business?

What type of business would you work in?

Do you want to have your own business?

What type of business would you create?

2009 © Ken Ninomiya . www.BizEBunch.com . www.rustyslemonadestand.com

Rusty thought about what Ms. Sam said in class. He also wanted to be a great American and wanted to start a new business. Rusty went home from school thinking about what type of business he would want to start.

Rusty thought about what he did really well and he thought about what he could make to sell in his business. He thought about teaching his friends how to play video games but he didn't think his Mom would let his friends come over after school. He thought about doing yard work for his Dad but Rusty was not strong enough yet to push the lawn mower.

Later that evening, Rusty's mom asked him to help with dinner and she gave him the chore of making lemonade. He was able to make the lemonade with no problem. His Mom said it was so good he could sell it. That was a great idea. Rusty would sell lemonade!

2009 © Ken Ninomiya . www.BizEBunch.com . www.rustyslemonadestand.com

After dinner Rusty told his Dad about his new business idea. His Dad thought that Rusty had a good idea to earn money and told him he would help him open his own lemonade business. Rusty's Dad called him an Entrepreneur. (pronounced "on-trah-prah-nor")

"Anyone can be an entrepreneur," his dad said. "Everyone can start a business if they work really hard at it."

Rusty asked his dad one more question before "lights out" that night. "Dad, what do I need to do to start the lemonade business and be an Entrepreneur ?"

An Entrepreneur is someone who has an idea and starts a business, just like Rusty's lemonade idea.

LEARN.

2009 © Ken Ninomiya . www.BizEBunch.com . www.rustyslemonadestand.com

The next morning, Rusty and his Mom went to the grocery store. Rusty's Mom let him add five lemons and a bag of sugar to the shopping list. These were important ingredients to make lemonade.

Mr. George, the grocery store manager, took the money from Rusty's mom as she paid for the groceries. Rusty told Mr. George that he was going to sell lemonade. Mr. George smiled and said, "That is great. You'll earn some money if your business makes a profit."

Mr. George explained that to make lemonade you need to spend money to buy the ingredients like lemons and sugar. The lemons and sugar cost your business money. You get to keep the extra money when you sell your lemonade for more then it cost you to make it. Mr. George called this "profit."

A business earns profit. Profit is the money a business gets to keep after it pays for everything it needs to operate the business.

LEARN.

2009 © Ken Ninomiya . www.BizEBunch.com . www.rustyslemonadestand.com

9

Rusty's Thinking Box

How much profit will Rusty make?
 Lets try to figure it out.

It costs $2.00 to make one
pitcher of Rusty's lemonade.
A pitcher of lemonade will
make 10 cups.

5 Lemons cost .20 cents each (5 x .20)		$1.00
Sugar costs $1.00	+	$1.00
It costs $2.00 to make lemonade	=	$2.00

Rusty will sell each cup of lemonade for 50 cents.
Rusty expects to sell 10 cups of lemonade and earn
$5.00 from each pitcher he sells. (.50 cents x 10 = $5.00)

Rusty makes $5.00 when he sells his lemonade, but it costs him
$2.00 to make his lemonade. How much profit does Rusty keep?

$5.00	total money earned by selling lemonade
- $2.00	total money it cost to make lemonade
=	total profit Rusty keeps

10

2009 © Ken Ninomiya . www.BizEBunch.com . www.rustyslemonadestand.com

2009 © Ken Ninomiya . www.BizEBunch.com . www.rustyslemonadestand.com

Rusty was now ready to start his lemonade business. He had all of the ingredients to make his lemonade. His Mom gave him a big plastic pitcher and ten plastic cups. Rusty's Mom gave his business a name : "Rusty's Lemonade Stand". Rusty's older sister Liz helped him to make a big sign. The sign read "Rusty's Lemonade Stand. Home Made. $.50 per cup."

Rusty and his Dad set out a table and a chair in front of his home. Rusty taped the sign to the front of the table. Rusty's Mom brought out a big cooler full of ice so that the lemonade would be ice-cold when Rusty sold it. Rusty's Lemonade stand was now in business.

2009 © Ken Ninomiya · www.BizEBunch.com · www.rustyslemonadestand.com

LEARN.

A customer is someone that buys something from a business. Without customers a business will not make money or earn profits.

Rusty waited patiently by his lemonade stand business for a few minutes until his neighbor Mr. Frank walked by to say hello.

"Hey, Rusty how is business?" Mr. Frank asked.

"Not good," Rusty said. "I have not sold any lemonade yet."

"Really?" Mr. Frank said. "Well, let me be your first customer."

"WOW! That's cool Mr. Frank," Rusty said with excitement.

"Please give me two cups of your lemonade. One for me now and one for me later. How much is that?" asked Mr. Frank.

"It is 50 cents per cup so that will be $1.00 total," calculated Rusty.

Mr. Frank gave Rusty a one dollar bill. Rusty was in business!

Rusty collected his first $1.00 from his lemonade stand business. He put it securely in his front pocket and waited for his next customer.

A short while later Rusty saw his Grandma and Grandpa drive up to the front of the house. Grandma walked over to him to give him a great big hug and kiss.

Grandma was happy to see that Rusty had his own lemonade stand. She was proud to see him trying to earn his own money. Grandma told Rusty to make sure that he gives everyone the same amount of lemonade in every cup and give each customer back their proper change from their money.

Grandma said that this is the honest and right thing to do. She called this being "ethical" in business. Grandma explained that a businessperson must be honest and fair. Rusty always listened to Grandma and Rusty wanted his business to always be ethical.

Grandma bought a cup of lemonade for 50 cents and sat next to Rusty to help his business.

2009 © Ken Ninomiya • www.BizEBunch.com • www.rustyslemonadestand.com

13

A few minutes later, the men who collect the garbage came down the street to collect the trash. One of them that saw Rusty every Saturday came over to his lemonade stand.

Rusty asked him if he owned his own trash collection business. The man told Rusty that the city owns the trash collection business. Rusty's Dad was right—anyone can own a business, even a city.

The man said that the city collects money from everyone who owns a business or works for a business. When the city collects this money it is called "taxes". The city uses taxes to run a business like collecting the garbage.

Rusty asked the man if he has to pay taxes. "Everyone has to pay taxes," the trash man said. "Please give me two cups of lemonade."

2009 © Ken Ninomiya . www.BizEBunch.com . www.rustyslemonadestand.com

14

Rusty's Grandpa came by to see how he was doing. He was proud to see that Rusty had his own lemonade business. He explained to Rusty that owning a business was called "capitalism" and this makes the U.S. great.

Grandpa explained that some people want to have their own business and some people want to work for a business. Grandpa explained that you can be really good at your own business and you can be really good at working, but you must do something you like to do and work very hard everyday.

"I must be good at business because I like to work hard every day," Rusty told his Grandpa.

"Well, you certainly do work hard. Now let's see how hard you worked to make your lemonade really tasty. Please give me two cups," Grandpa said.

Grandpa drank both cups of Rusty's lemonade and he went back into the house.

Capitalism allows anyone to own a business and keep the money they earn from working. This is how we live in the United States.

LEARN.

2009 © Ken Ninomiya • www.BizEBunch.com • www.rustyslemonadestand.com

It was getting close to lunch time and Rusty's belly was starting to rumble for food. Rusty's Dad and his sister Liz came by to visit him at his lemonade stand.

Rusty was very happy to see his Dad and his sister. Rusty's Dad asked him , "How was business?" Rusty said that having a lemonade stand business was tough but he liked to earn his own money and he is working hard.

2009 © Ken Ninomiya . www.BizEBunch.com . www.rustyslemonadestand.com

"I am very proud of you", Rusty's Dad told him. "You did a great job of getting everything organized for your lemonade stand ."

"Well..." Rusty said. "Liz helped me, Mommy helped me, and even you helped me, Daddy. So my whole family helped me".

"Well. That is true. All of your family helped you," Dad said. "Your family is the most important part of your life. When you have a business your family may be part of it. You have to keep this in mind when you become a very successful businessman. Your family is more important than your business. They will always be there for you."

16

Rusty was happy his Dad said that, because he was so, so, so, soooo tired and he really needed their help to take down the lemonade stand.

"OK, Rusty. Let's go have some lunch. Can I buy your last three cups of tasty lemonade? I'll take one for me, one for your sister and one for you because you worked so hard."

"Ok," Rusty said and he poured the last three cups with equal amounts in each. He used up all of the ice that was in the cooler to make the lemonade really cold.

Rusty's Dad took out $1.50 from his wallet and gave it to Rusty. Rusty put the money in his front pocket with all of the other money he collected that day from his lemonade stand business.

Rusty, Liz and their Dad shared the last three cups of Rusty's Homemade Lemonade just before they went into the house for lunch. Together, they cleaned up all of the things Rusty used for his lemonade stand business and packed it neatly to carry back to the house.

2009 © Ken Ninomiya . www.BizEBunch.com . www.rustyslemonadestand.com

17

Rusty counted the money he earned selling lemonade after lunch. The total was $5.00 and Rusty remembered that it cost $2.00 to buy the ingredients to make the lemonade. Rusty calculated that his profit for the day was $3.00.

Rusty sold a pitcher of lemonade everyday for the next four days. He earned a total of $15.00 in five days by selling lemonade. Rusty added the $15.00 he earned to the $15.00 he already had saved up from his allowance. Rusty did it! He had $30.00 to buy the new video game!

Rusty's Dad took him to the store to buy the video game and it made Rusty feel very proud that he earned his money by being an entrepreneur. Rusty and his Dad walked out of the video game store when Rusty said, "I wonder what is the next business I can do to earn money?"

"How about a car wash?" Rusty's Dad said. Rusty thought about how many cars he could wash to earn more money. Maybe that could be his next business!

2009 © Ken Ninomiya · www.BizEBunch.com · www.rustyslemonadestand.com

New Words

Allowance – This is money that you get from your Mom & Dad for doing your chores, doing well in school and being on your best behavior.

Boss – This is the person that is responsible for a business. They make the daily decisions on what to do to help build the business.

Ethical – When you do not lie, cheat or steal you are being ethical. If you do something that is fair and does not hurt someone you are being ethical.

Fair – This means that you do not do something just for yourself and you consider others.

Honest – You do not lie, cheat or steal from others.

Manager – A person who helps to operate a business. Sometimes a business has many managers that are responsible for different parts of the business.

Sell – When you offer something to someone in exchange for money, you sell it to them. In a business you sell products or services to earn money.

Taxes– Most people and businesses pay the government money to help build streets, schools and more. The taxes that are collected help to run cities in the USA.

RUSTY'S
Lemonade Stand
Home Made
50¢ /cup

19

2009 © Ken Ninomiya . www.BizEBunch.com . www.rustyslemonadestand.com

Rusty's Thinking Box

Let's Make Business Cards!

A business card helps everyone know who you are and what your business does. Write your name on the blank line. Have your Mom and Dad help you to carefully cut out each card. Hand out your business cards to all of your customers.

Carefully cut out each card above. Have your parents help you with the scissors.

_____
Write your name above.
Fresh Made Lemonade.

Only 50 Cents per cup!

_____
Write your name above.
Fresh Made Lemonade.

Only 50 Cents per cup!

_____
Write your name above.
Fresh Made Lemonade.

Only 50 Cents per cup!

_____
Write your name above.
Fresh Made Lemonade.

Only 50 Cents per cup!

_____
Write your name above.
Fresh Made Lemonade.

Only 50 Cents per cup!

_____
Write your name above.
Fresh Made Lemonade.

Only 50 Cents per cup!

_____
Write your name above.
Fresh Made Lemonade.

Only 50 Cents per cup!

_____
Write your name above.
Fresh Made Lemonade.

Only 50 Cents per cup!

2009 © Ken Ninomiya . www.BizEBunch.com . www.RustysLemonadestand.com

Rusty's Thinking Box

RUSTY'S Lemonade Stand Home Made

50¢ /cup

Lemonade Recipe
Ingredients:
5 Lemons
1 cup of sugar
1 Gallon of water
Ice to serve in
cups

Recipe to make great homemade lemonade.

Have your Mom or Dad help you with this.

1. Get a 1 gallon water pitcher from Mom or Dad

2. Have Mom or Dad cut the 5 lemons in half for you.
   NEVER USE A KNIFE WITHOUT YOUR MOM OR DAD!

3. Squeeze the lemons into the pitcher. Squeeze out all of the juice!
   Put the squeezed lemons into the pitcher when done.
   MOM AND DAD CAN HELP YOU WITH THIS ALSO!

4. Pour the cup of sugar into pitcher.

5. Fill the pitcher with cold water. Stir everything up.
   BE CAREFUL NOT TO FILL IT UP TOO MUCH.
   MOM AND DAD CAN HELP YOU WITH THIS ALSO.

6. When ready to drink, put a little ice in a plastic cup and pour
   the lemonade into the cup. DRINK IT UP!
   MOM AND DAD CAN HELP YOU POUR THE LEMONADE.

2009 © Ken Ninomiya . www.BizEBunch.com . www.rustyslemonadestand.com

Rusty's Thinking Box

Let's write a business plan to help you create your own
Lemonade Stand Business. Write an answer for each blank below.
Use the hints below each blank line to write your answer.

The name of my business will be _____ Lemonade Stand.
Write in your business name here.

The address of my business is _____.
Write in your city and state here.

My business will sell homemade lemonade and _____.
Write in what other food you may want to sell.

I will sell my lemonade for 50 cents per cup.

My goal is to sell _____ cups of lemonade.
Write in how many cups of lemonade you want to sell.

I will ask _____ to help me.
Write in who will need to help you start your business.

I want to make enough money to buy _____.
Write in what you want buy when you make a profit.

I will ask _____ for money to start my business.
Write in who will need to give you money to start your business.

I will need $_____ to start my business.
Write in how much money you will need to start your business. Remember you need to buy ingredients!

I will pay back _____ the money that they give me.
Write in the name of the person who gave you money to start your business.

Rusty's Thinking Box

Let's Make A Business Sign!

Write in your name or your business name on the top of the sign.
Have Mom and Dad help you to cut out the sign. Use tape to hang.

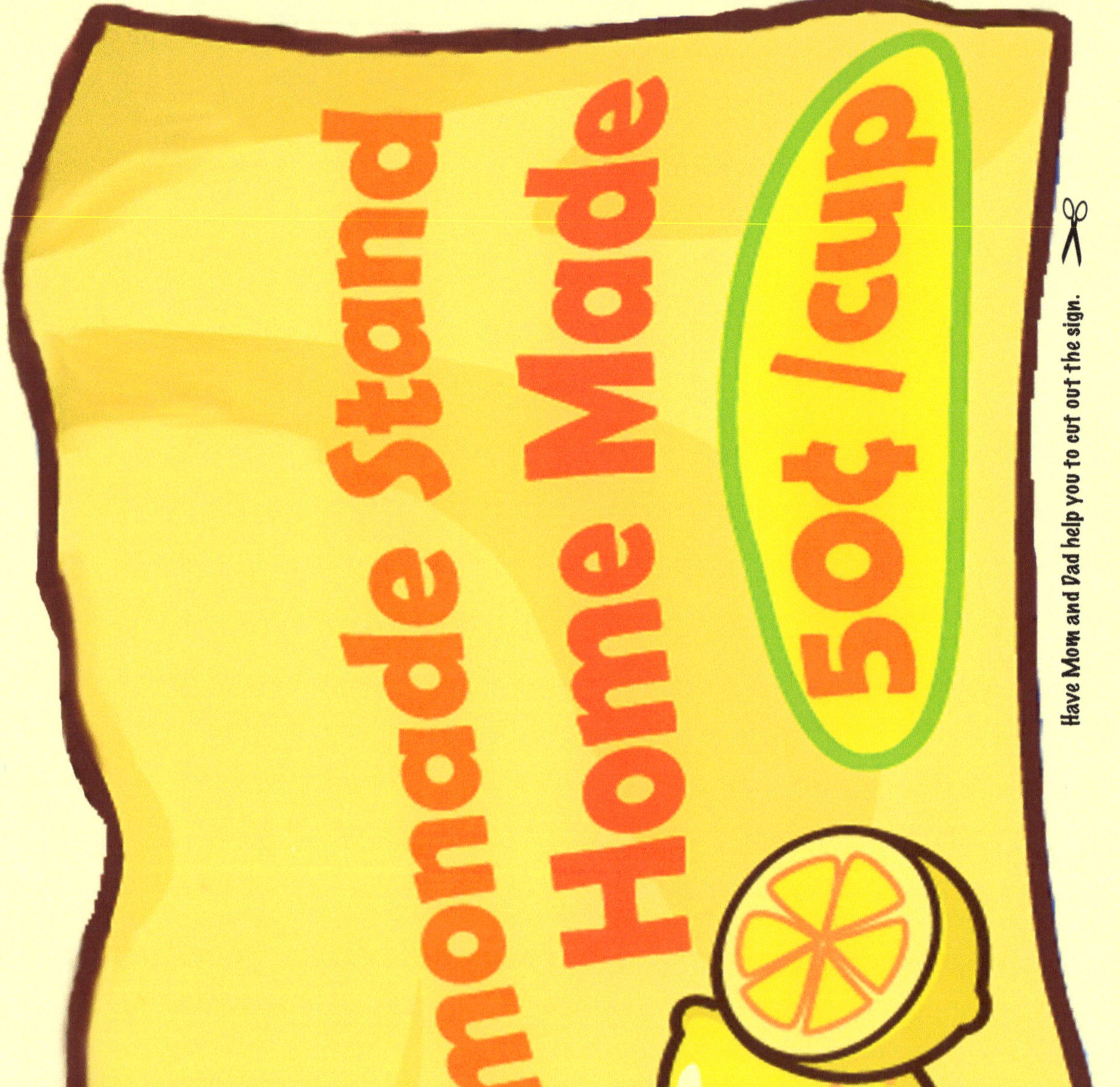
Lemonade Stand
Home Made
50¢ /cup

Have Mom and Dad help you to cut out the sign.

2009 © Ken Ninomiya . www.BizEBunch.com . www.RustysLemonadestand.com

Let's Discuss Goals.

When you say, "I want to..." you are starting to think of a goal. Your goal might be that you want start your business or learn how to play your favorite video game better. Having goals are important because it helps you to concentrate on completing your idea.

Every one should have goals. A business will be more successful when it has a goal. Rusty's business goal was to sell enough cups of lemonade to buy the new video game. His business was a success when he accomplished his goal.

Do you have a goal right now? Do you want to do something in the future? What are you doing to help you reach your goal?

Use the space below to write down three goals.

1. I want to _____

_____

_____

2. _____

_____

_____

3. _____

_____

_____

How do I reach my goals?

Now that you have written three goals, lets discuss how you can reach your goals. When you think of a goal it should always be something that you can do with a little extra effort. You will have to work harder to reach your goals. You will have to write a plan to reach your goals.

Rusty's goal was to get enough money to buy a new video game. To help him reach his goal he started a lemonade business. Rusty had to buy the ingredients, make a sign and sit outside to sell his lemonade. All of these actions were part of the plan Rusty had to do to reach his goal.

You will have to make a plan that will help you reach your goals. Write down two actions for each of your goals that will help you reach them.

To reach goal #1 my plan is to do these two actions:

☑ _____

_____

To reach goal #2 my plan is to do these two actions:

☑ _____

_____

To reach goal #3 my plan is to do these two actions:

☑ _____

_____

2009 © Ken Ninomiya . www.BizEBunch.com . www.RustysLemonadestand.com

My idea for a business!

Rusty's Lemonade Stand was a huge success! He reached his goal and earned enough of his own money to buy a new video game.

Rusty wanted to come up with new ideas for a business. Can you help him?
Think about something that you do now that you can make a business out of. Do you draw well? Maybe you can sell your drawings. Do you know how to bake cookies? You can sell your special cookies! Are you good at math? Maybe you can be a tutor!

The most important part of coming up with a new business idea is to help people get something that they need and want. When you think of your idea make sure that you can think of why someone would want to buy something from your business. Use the space below to come up with a new business idea.

_____

_____

_____

_____

_____

_____

Rusty's Thinking Box

Can you find these words? Circle each one as you find it.

```
F A M E L E E M O M E R T D E C A S T E R F O Z
A A L L O Q W P O L T I K L R E U M I D E R O A M
M L M B E N T R E P R E N E U R H S T O V O I N B
L I I I M A F O F I T G R M O R T H T G E W N B I
E O X O L O O F I B H T M O N E Y I G O R F B T O
E W O O E Y K I N I E P Z N O T H I N K M M V O U
T A X E S E H T A Z T O M A N A G E R D O E O S S
T N S A L L E S T E O C U D A V I R S O N N R U A
E C M O N I T E E B U S I E T H I C S K E T O S L
M E R B T O R P R U R E S E N O R T S A T R B A L
W O K R L B U S I N E S S E J A N N A M L E O F
A M B U T O U S I C A P I T A L I S M N R E F L S
U S T A A S A Y O H O N E S T Y T O N I Y R S E
```

ALLOWANCE

AMBITOUS

BIZEBUNCH

BUSINESS

CAPITALISM

CUSTOMER

ENTREPRENEUR

ETHICS

FAMILY

HONESTY

LEMONADE

MANAGER

MONEY

SALES

TAXES

 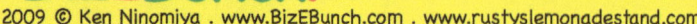 2009 © Ken Ninomiya . www.BizEBunch.com . www.rustyslemonadestand.com

Rusty's Thinking Box

Test yourself with this BizEBunch Quiz. Circle the best answer.

Rusty's Lemonade Worldwide Sales

1. What is a business?

a) A place where people work.
b) A place where I can play.
c) A place to go to sleep.

2. Who can own a business?

a) Everybody! Even me.
b) Nobody can own a business.
c) Only the government can own a business.

How many can you get right?
Check your answers on Page 29.
Go on line to www.BizEBunch.com
to get your achievement certificate.

3. Can I own a business as a kid?

a) Yes -if a grown-up helps me.
b) No - only grown ups own a business.
c) No - kids are not allowed to own a business.

4. Are you the "boss" if you own a business?

a) Yes. A business owner must be responsible for everything for their business.
b) No. You do not do important things if you own a business.
c) No. A business does not have a boss.

5. Do I need to learn about business so that I can own a business?

a) Yes. You should learn about business so that you can be successful
b) No. You should just try to own a business. without studying about it.
c) No. A business is real easy to own.

  **28**

Rusty's Thinking Box

Answer Page

Word Search - Page 27

```
F A M E L E E M O M E R T D E C A S T E R F O Z
F A L L O Q W P O L T I K L R E U M I D E R O A
M L M B E N T R E P R E N E U R H S T O V O I M
L L I I M A F O F I T G R M O R T H T G E W N B
E O X O L O O F I B H T M O N E Y I G O R F B I
E W O O E Y K I N I E P Z N O T H I N K M M V T
T A X E S E H T A Z T O M A N A G E R D O E D O
T N S A L L E S T E O C U D A V I R S O N N R U
E C M O N I T E E B U S I E T H I C S K E T O S
M E R B T O R P R U R E S E N O R T S A T R B A
W O K R L B U S I N E S S E J A N N A M L E O L
A M B U T O U S I C A P I T A L I S M N R E F L
U S T A A S A Y O H O N E S T Y T O N I Y R S E
```

BizEBunch Quiz - Page 28

Print your **BizEBunch** Achievement Certificate on line! Go to **WWW.BizEBunch.com** to sign up.

You must have your parents permission and e-mail address to register.

1. **What is a business?**
   a) A place where people work.

2. **Who can own a business?**
   a) Everybody! Even me.

3. **Can I own a business as a kid?**
   a) Yes - if a grown-up helps me.

4. **Are you the "boss" if you own a business?**
   a) Yes. A business owner must be responsible for everything for their business.

5. **Do I need to learn about business so that I can own a business?**
   a) Yes. You should learn about business so that you can be successful.

29

2009 © Ken Ninomiya . www.BizEBunch.com . www.rustyslemonadestand.com

Do **YOU** have what it takes to be in this **bunch?**

BizEBunch.com

Become a member of the BizEBunch Team today!
FREE TEAM MEMBERSHIP registration online.

✔ **FREE Membership includes:**
Access to all FREE online material, tools and games.
FREE E-book previews of future BizEBunch books.
Special offers from BizEBunch and our partners.
Three new BizEBunch on line work sheets per month.
Team membership discounts on all BizEBunch items.
Advice for kids and parents.
New Features monthly!

Go to **www.BizEBunch.com** to sign up. You must have
your parents permission and e-mail address to register.
See membership registration on-line for more details.

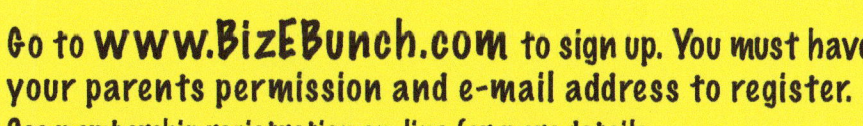

Suki's Short Summer
by Ken Ninomiya

READ. LEARN. Do.

www.ingramcontent.com/pod-product-compliance
Lightning Source LLC
Chambersburg PA
CBHW041604120626
46551CB00002B/308